A Cardinal's First Game

Story © 2011, Erin Callier and Daniel McCarthy
Art © 2011, Daniel McCarthy

Major League Baseball trademarks and copyrights are used
with permission of Major League Baseball Properties, Inc.

Printed in the United States.

PRT0911B

ISBN-13: 978-1-936319-34-3
ISBN-10: 1-936319-34-9

Mascot Books
560 Herndon Parkway #120, Herndon, VA 20170

www.mascotbooks.com

A Cardinal's First Game

Written by
Erin Callier and Daniel McCarthy

Illustrated by
Daniel McCarthy

There weren't many things Louie liked to do more than to explore. From the moment he took his first flight from the nest, he was hooked on discovering new places and seeing all there was for a little bird to see.

While out exploring one early spring morning, Louie found a mysterious item that he just couldn't figure out…

What were the cardinal birds doing on that man's shirt? Were they famous? Were they explorers, too?

Paper in tow, Louie flew to the nest as fast as his little wings would take him.

"Mama! Papa! Look what I found! What does it mean?" Louie asked in a rush.

"That looks like *Cardinals* baseball to me," said Papa Cardinal.

"Baseball? What's that?" Louie asked.

"Baseball's a game where people try to make a ball soar, just like a bird," Papa Cardinal explained. "The St. Louis team is called the *Cardinals* because their uniforms have the same color red as our feathers," Papa Cardinal said proudly.

"Papa, you should take Louie to the game today," said Mama Cardinal.

Louie flapped his wings in excitement. "Please, Papa? Please? Can we go to the game?"

"I can't think of a finer way to spend the afternoon," said Papa.

As they flew from the nest, Papa taught Louie everything he knew about baseball. From home runs to hot dogs to double plays, Papa told Louie all the rules of America's National Pastime.

"Do you think the *Cardinals* will score a home run today?" Louie asked.

"I sure hope so," said Papa Cardinal. "At the very least, there will definitely be hot dogs. And peanuts. And cotton candy."

"I like baseball already!" Louie exclaimed.

In no time at all, Louie and Papa Cardinal were soaring into downtown St. Louis. Louie was amazed at all the sights before him.

Giant buildings, the Mississippi River, shimmering fountains, and even a mighty arch towering above it all.

"Papa, we should build ourselves a nest at the very top!" Louie shouted, pointing his wing toward the great Gateway Arch.

"That would certainly be one fine view!" said Papa.

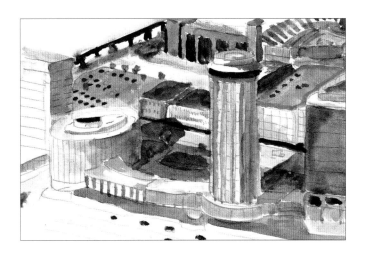

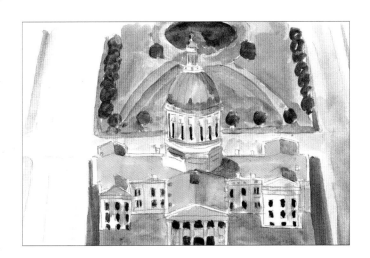

"And that, Louie, is *Busch Stadium*™. Home of the *St. Louis Cardinals*," Papa Cardinal said as they flew over the stadium and a sea of fans dressed in cardinal red.

"It's kind of shaped like a giant nest, Papa!" Louie shouted as they swooped down towards the crowded stadium.

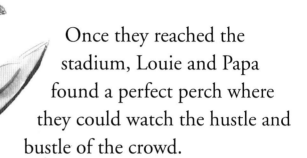

Once they reached the stadium, Louie and Papa found a perfect perch where they could watch the hustle and bustle of the crowd.

"Who's that man?" Louie asked of the bronze statue just outside the stadium.

"That, Louie, is 'The Man'," Papa Cardinal said with a smile. "Stan 'The Man' Musial. One of the best baseball players the game has ever known."

"And he was a player for the *Cardinals*?" Louie asked in amazement.

"Yep. For his entire career!" answered Papa.

As Louie and Papa Cardinal ventured into the stadium, Louie was stunned by all the wonders that surrounded them. All the people, excitement, and, yes, cotton candy that Papa had promised was there, and then some.

Louie just couldn't resist helping himself to a french fry from a vendor before Papa led the way to their seats.

"Hurry! We don't want to miss the first pitch," Papa said.

Perched between third base and home plate, Louie was in awe of the vast green field and the St. Louis skyline before them.

"Louie, do you remember what I told you about baseball during our flight over?" Papa asked during the first inning.

"Well, the *Cardinals* are at bat, soooo…that means our player has three chances to hit the ball where the other team can't catch it before it hits the ground," said Louie. "Then, if he does that, he has to run to all the bases faster than the other team can throw it there, right?"

"Right," said Papa. "Then, if he makes it back to home plate, the *Cardinals* score a run."

As the *Cardinals* tried their best to score, Louie was eager to get a closer look…

Before Papa could notice, Louie zoomed toward the *Cardinals* dugout in search of some action.

As he watched the team, Louie noticed one man who appeared to be the Papa Cardinal making strange gestures with his hands. Pointing to his nose, tugging on his ear, tapping his hip. What a sight!

Remembering what Papa told him during their flight, Louie knew this meant he was sending secret signals to the *Cardinals* player standing at bat.

Soon, Papa found Louie in the dugout. Annoyed with Louie for taking off without him, Papa scolded him, "It's one thing to go off exploring on your own at home, but a little bird like you could get lost in such a big crowd!"

"You're right, Papa," Louie said sheepishly. "I won't do it again. But… now that you're here, do you think we can get an even closer look?"

The remaining innings flew by. It was a close game, and in the bottom of the ninth, the *Cardinals* won with a soaring home run, just like Louie had hoped.

Fireworks erupted with a bang and all the *Cardinals* fans were on their feet, clapping and shouting wildly for the home team.

After the celebration was over, Papa and Louie flew towards home, chirping their own happy version of "*Take Me Out To The Ballgame*™" all the way.

Once they returned to their nest, Louie gave Mama Cardinal a play-by-play of the game and all that he and Papa had seen on their ballpark adventure.

Finally, exhausted from the day's excitement, Louie fell into a sleep filled with dreams of freshly cut grass, the crack of the bat, and the unmistakable smell of peanuts.

The End